Some Swahili Words

Ahadi
promise, agreement

Boma
fortress

Kopa
heart

Pimbi
hyrax

Rafiki
friend

Shenzi
savage, rude

Taka
want, rubbish

Uru
diamonds

Zuzu
inexperienced

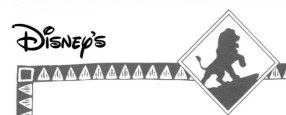

Disney's

THE
LION KING

A TALE OF TWO BROTHERS

by Alex Simmons

Illustrations by Denise Shimabukuro
Raymond Zibach

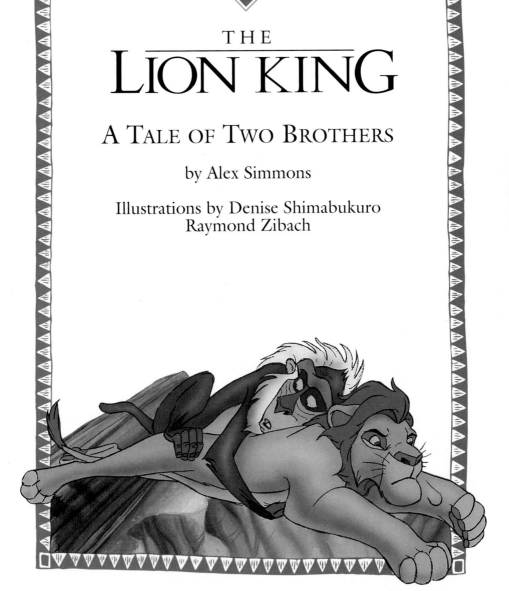

©1994 The Walt Disney Company. No portion of this book may be reproduced without written consent of The Walt Disney Company. Produced by Mega-Books, Inc. Design and art direction by Michaelis/Carpelis Design Assoc., Inc.
Printed in the United States of America.

Grolier Books

ISBN: 0-7172-8348-8

CHAPTER 1

Gotcha!" Kopa leaped through the air at his target, a hyrax named Pimbi. Perfect, Kopa thought, just perfect.

But Pimbi moved.

Kopa landed in the dirt with a thud. "Rats!" he muttered.

Pimbi shook with laughter. "You'll never catch me that way," he said. "Some king you'll make."

Kopa shook the dust from his soft golden fur. "Shows how much you know," he said. "Someday I'll rule the Pride Lands!" Kopa's father was Simba, the Lion King.

Pimbi giggled. "Not if you don't learn to pounce better."

"My dad said he would give me more lessons. Then I'll—" Kopa froze. "I just remembered something," he shouted. "My dad promised to show me something special today!"

"What?" Pimbi asked.

"I'll tell you about it tomorrow," Kopa said as he headed for home. "See you then!"

Kopa ran up the base of a rocky hill. This was Pride Rock, the tallest spot in all of the Pride Lands.

Kopa couldn't help smiling. His father had promised to show him the kingdom from the top of Pride Rock.

"My father took me there when I was a cub," Simba had told Kopa. "It's a tradition."

Kopa had never met his *babu*, his grandfather, Mufasa. But he had heard about him from his father's steward, the hornbill Zazu, and the older animals.

They all said Mufasa had been a great king.

Now Simba, son of Mufasa, was the Lion King. Kopa thought his father was a great king, too, even though it kept him busy. So busy that Simba hadn't been able to spend much time with Kopa.

But today would be different.

When Kopa reached the ledge where his family slept, his mother, Nala, was lying on a flat rock overlooking the grassy plain below.

"Did you have fun with Pimbi?" Nala asked.

Kopa skidded to a stop and cocked his head. "How did you know what I was doing?" he asked.

Nala licked his face. "You are never far from my sight or my protection," she replied. "I can see everything that moves on the plain."

Kopa frowned. "Creepy."

At that moment, Simba bounded up onto the ledge, followed by Zazu and

Rafiki, a wise old baboon.

Zazu was chattering. "The crocodiles are snapping at everybody. The hippos are throwing their weight around . . . ."

"Crisis at the water hole again," Nala told Kopa.

"Calm down, Zazu," Rafiki said. He turned to Simba. "What he's trying to say is, the animals are not sharing the water. By rights, all should—"

"Dad!" Kopa dashed over to Simba. "I'm ready to go!"

Simba nuzzled Kopa with his nose, then looked up at Rafiki. "Isn't there something you and Zazu can do about this crisis?" he asked.

Rafiki shook his head. "No, Young King."

"I've tried," Zazu said. "But no one will listen to me."

Simba sighed. "Sorry, son. But I can't take you to the summit now."

"But you promised, Dad," Kopa said softly. "You promised."

"Try to understand," Nala said to Kopa. "Your father has serious responsibilities. The other animals need that water supply."

Kopa lowered his head. "He promised."

Simba turned to Rafiki. "Maybe you could explain how important this crisis is."

"Ah, but I agree with the little one," Rafiki said. "A promise has great value. Kingdoms have suffered when promises were broken."

Simba tilted his head to one side. "But I thought—"

"Sit, Kopa," said Rafiki. "Let me tell you a tale of a king, a prince, and a great enemy."

Kopa jumped with excitement. "Is the enemy a hairy giant with purple eyes?"

"No," Rafiki said. "But he does have a scar down his left cheek."

Simba, Nala, and Zazu knew who Rafiki was talking about. It was Scar,

Simba's uncle. He had killed Kopa's grandfather, Mufasa.

Simba had been a cub when Mufasa was killed. Simba had run away, thinking that he was responsible for his father's death.

Timon, a meerkat, and Pumbaa, a warthog, had rescued Simba. They had lived together in a faraway jungle until Nala had come looking for Simba. She had told him that Scar was ruling the Pride Lands with the hyenas as his helpers. The other animals were suffering because Scar was not ruling wisely. Simba had consented to go back to the Pride Lands and claim his rightful place as the Lion King.

Simba's battle with Scar had been fierce and deadly. But he had won. Simba thought all that was behind him. Now Rafiki was about to reveal some secret about his grandfather, his father, and his evil uncle.

CHAPTER 2

"In those days, the Pride Lands were in deep trouble," Rafiki said.

"A drought lay upon the earth, which had turned to dust. The animals were fighting not just for water but for food and space.

"This was the land that I, Rafiki, wandered into. . . ."

Rafiki had been traveling for many hours. He was hot and tired.

A colorful hornbill flew over Rafiki. "You look pooped," she called. "Why don't you sit down in the shade?" She landed at his feet.

"I would love to, Miss, uh, Miss . . ." Rafiki began.

"Zuzu is the name," she replied. "There's shade over that hill, at Five Stones," she said. "Well, have to fly. So much to do, so little time." She took to the air and flew out of sight.

Rafiki found Five Stones easily. In fact, it was the only shade for miles around, five egg-shaped boulders lying together, as though they were in a giant nest.

But as Rafiki approached Five Stones, he had the feeling he was being watched. He turned to see three grinning hyenas racing toward him.

"Lunch!" one of them shouted.

Rafiki backed up against a boulder and raised his staff, though it would have been of little defense against them.

As they were closing in, Rafiki heard a mighty roar. The hyenas froze.

Rafiki looked up and saw a lion on the rocks above him. He had a long black mane and bright green eyes. It was

Ahadi, the Lion King. Two young lions were with him. One seemed ready to fight. The other looked bored.

"You have eaten already," Ahadi told the hyenas.

Two of the hyenas bowed their heads and trembled. "Yes, sire," they said. The third hyena covered his head with his front paws and giggled.

The female hyena grinned at the king. "But Ahadi"—her voice was scratchy—"there wasn't much meat on that little—"

"Silence, Shenzi!" Ahadi said. "You were going to kill for sport. That is not permitted in the Pride Lands. Now, go!"

The hyenas ran off.

"You really should have let them have the old fellow," the bored lion said. He jumped down and circled Rafiki. "Though I suspect the meat would be tough even for me."

"Leave him alone, Taka," said the other young lion. He jumped down beside Rafiki. "My name is Mufasa. This rude one is my brother. And this is our father, Ahadi, the Lion King."

"What brings you to the Pride Lands?" Ahadi asked Rafiki.

"I am Rafiki, and I search for knowledge," he replied. "I study the African land—its magic, its myths, its legends. I have learned much about the healing properties of plants."

Taka yawned, "How exciting."

"You might profit from such a quest," said Ahadi.

Taka growled.

"I would like to speak to you about our troubles," Ahadi said to Rafiki. "Perhaps your knowledge might be of some help."

Rafiki followed the Lion King and his sons back to Pride Rock. Taka wandered off. Ahadi told Rafiki that his mate, Uru, was away, hunting for a new source of food and water.

Rafiki and Ahadi talked for many hours. When darkness came, Ahadi invited Rafiki to stay the night. Rafiki made a bed of leaves on the ledge where the lions slept.

The Pride Lands below the ledge were vast. The grass would have gone on forever, but it was interrupted by dried water holes, rocks, and here and there, stretches of trees. In the distance, the blue hills were vanishing into the sky as night fell. The mighty Zuberi River was only a silver stream in the moonlight.

"I like to sleep under the stars," Rafiki said to Mufasa, "and talk to the wise ones of the past."

Mufasa stretched out beside Rafiki on the ledge. "I talk to the Lion Kings of old, who also live among the stars."

"Does your brother do this too?" Rafiki asked. "He is not home yet."

"No," Mufasa said. "Taka doesn't like to do much of anything. He and my father don't get along." Mufasa rested his head on his front paws. "Taka doesn't like me much either."

"Do you like him?" Rafiki asked.

"He is my younger brother," Mufasa sighed. "I look after him."

After a bit, Rafiki and Mufasa said good night, and in a short while, they were fast asleep.

But Rafiki's slumber was disturbed. Something rustled the leaves of his bed. When he opened his eyes, a spitting cobra was facing him. The snake's eyes sparkled in the moonlight, and his hood was spread wide. He was ready to strike.

CHAPTER

"id the snake bite you?" Kopa asked.

"No, Young Prince," Rafiki replied. "The cobra did not bite. He spit."

Kopa wrinkled his face. "Gross."

"May I continue my tale?" Rafiki asked. When Kopa nodded eagerly, Rafiki went on.

Mufasa awoke seconds after Rafiki did. The moment Mufasa saw the danger, he rose to his feet.

"Don't move," Rafiki whispered.

"But—"

"Quiet," Rafiki said, never looking away from the cobra.

Rafiki stared into the snake's eyes—deeper and deeper, filling his mind with calm, friendly thoughts.

"We are not enemies," he told the cobra. "We are part of the great circle of life." The snake began to sway from side to side. "We are not enemies," he kept repeating. "We are brothers. We must live in harmony with all living things on earth."

The cobra folded his cowl, relaxed, then slithered down the hill. Rafiki let out a deep breath.

Mufasa was at Rafiki's side in an instant. "How did you do that?" he asked.

"I learned it from an ancient baboon in Grass Walls, a land far away."

"But if the cobra had—"

Rafiki put his hand on Mufasa's strong shoulder. "But he didn't, and I am fine. Let us sleep."

Mufasa glanced around the ledge. Finally he lay down.

"Funny," he said. "There are snakes in the rocks above us, but they don't normally come down to the ledge. Especially at night, when it's cold."

"Who can truly say what a snake will do?" Rafiki said as he stretched out on his bed.

"I guess you're right." Mufasa yawned.

For a long time, Rafiki lay there wondering why he had not told Mufasa of his suspicion that someone had pushed the snake onto his bed. Maybe as a joke. Maybe not.

And he had noticed a strong scent in the air. A familiar scent. Perhaps Mufasa hadn't noticed it because he was used to the smell of his brother.

Two snakes have visited us tonight, thought Rafiki. And one of them was Taka.

The following morning, Rafiki awoke

before everyone else and set off to seek breakfast on the plain.

Many of the trees were bare. Giraffes, monkeys, and other plant eaters had picked them clean. But Rafiki managed to find some tiny leaves at the top of a tall tree. He was finishing his meal when he heard voices below.

Three hyenas had gathered at the base of the tree. They were the same ones that had attacked Rafiki the day before.

"I'm tired of Ahadi bossing us around, Banzai," said the one called Shenzi. "Who does he think he is?"

"The king, the boss, the top cat," Banzai replied.

The third hyena snickered.

"You think that's funny, Ed?" Shenzi said. She turned and casually flicked a piece of rotten meat into Banzai's face.

Ed snickered again.

"You know what I mean, Banzai," Shenzi snarled. "He's always spoiling our fun."

"Well, things are going to change," Banzai said, wiping his face. "Then nothing will stand in our way."

Rafiki didn't like the tone of Banzai's voice. There is more to these creatures than anyone suspects, he thought.

"Ahadi won't live forever," Shenzi said. Banzai nodded. "And if something happened to Mufasa"—"Hee-hee-hee," Ed snickered—"we'd be top dogs around here."

"Hyenas," Banzai said.

Shenzi flashed her sharp teeth. "One day," she said, "we'll hunt wherever, whenever, and whatever we want. The Pride Lands will be ours."

"Hee-hee-hee!"

CHAPTER

Rafiki's mind was racing. What were
they planning? he wondered.
Whatever they had in mind, he
knew it meant trouble for Ahadi and his
family.

The moment Shenzi and her com-
panions wandered off, Rafiki hurried back
to Pride Rock. He was anxious to tell
Ahadi what he had overheard.

But when he arrived, Ahadi was facing
a different crisis. Giraffes, zebras, wart-
hogs, and other animals were shouting,
stomping their feet, and complaining.
Mufasa sat at his father's side. Taka was
lying on the ground, a few feet away.

"There are hardly any leaves left, thanks to the giraffes," said an antelope.

"They're greedy," said a zebra. "That's the long and the short of it!"

"Not everything is black and white," said a giraffe. He pointed his nose in the air. "We need to eat too."

"What about water?" a leopard snarled. "There's only one water hole left, and Boma and the other Cape buffaloes won't let me near it."

A nervous ostrich plucked at her own feathers. "What about those nasty hyenas? They frighten me and my children."

"That's right," said a familiar voice. Rafiki looked up and saw Zuzu sitting in a tree. "They're attacking everything that moves, the monkeys, the oxpeckers, the springboks, the gazelles, the—"

"*Asante sana*. Thank you, Zuzu," Ahadi said. "I'll deal with the hyenas—"

"When?" asked the ostrich. "They're skulking around the only food sources we have."

"Right now," Ahadi declared.

"Oh, father, dear"—Taka was studying his claws—"didn't you promise to take me, uh, Mufasa and me, hunting this morning?" Taka eyed the ostrich, then licked his lips.

"Yes, I did," said Ahadi. "But I'm afraid it will have to wait."

Taka sprang to his feet. "I'm tired of waiting!" he snarled. "Something more important always comes up when you're supposed to take me somewhere."

"That's not true," said Ahadi. "Besides, being the Lion King carries great responsibilities." Ahadi glanced at Mufasa. "Your brother seems to understand these things."

"Mufasa gets all the attention!" Taka shouted. "After all, Daddy's favorite is going to be the next Lion King."

"Watch how you speak to me," Mufasa warned his brother.

"What about our problems?" called a parrot. "What about food and water? It

doesn't matter who wears the crown if we starve to death!"

The chattering went on like a great wall of noise. Ahadi threw back his head and roared, "Enough!" Everyone grew silent.

"I'll do what I can about the hyenas," Ahadi said. "But I have no control over the weather. I cannot make it rain. Uru is out searching for a new source of water and food for us. We must be patient until she returns."

Ahadi spoke softly to Taka. "Please try to understand."

"You broke your promise," Taka said. His eyes blazed. Rafiki felt certain he would begin roaring at the top of his lungs.

But the anger vanished like a cloud from the sun. Taka grinned and turned to Mufasa. "How about you and I go hunting by ourselves instead? It's better than nothing. We'll have some fun. Real fun." He laughed.

kept to the treetops, moving from limb to limb.

Finally, Taka stopped by a small dry water hole. Rafiki couldn't tell whether he was deep in thought or brooding with disappointment.

Taka stiffened. Three snarling hyenas leaped out of the bushes.

It was Shenzi, Banzai, and their giggling companion, Ed. They inched toward Taka, their heads low, the morning sun flashing on their deadly white teeth.

CHAPTER 5

"Please drop the dramatics," Taka said. He walked over to them.

They began to laugh.

"We had you worried for a minute, didn't we?" Shenzi said.

Taka rolled his eyes. "Oh, my fur turned white with fear. Now, listen up, you idiots."

The hyenas stopped laughing and became attentive.

"My father is looking for you," Taka continued. "So lie low until things cool off."

"I could sure use some cool weather," Banzai said. "Maybe we should move into the high mountains, where there's snow and—"

Taka and Shenzi yanked Banzai's whiskers.

"Ouch!" he cried.

Ed snickered.

"What did I do? What did I do?" Banzai asked.

Taka groomed one of his paws. "No wonder you begged me to join your little gang."

"Hey, who begged who?" Banzai snapped.

"He's right," Shenzi said.

Ed jiggled his head in agreement.

Taka raised his paw and released his long claws. "What were you saying?"

Banzai trembled. "It's a good thing we asked you to join us," he said.

Taka grinned.

Shenzi sneered, "I thought you were supposed to be hunting with your daddy."

"Plans were changed," Taka replied.

"He ditched you again?" she said.

"No one ditches me!" Taka roared.

The hyenas fell over one another trying to back away from Taka.

"Of course not!" Shenzi said as Taka backed them into a tree. "It's just that you said he was always choosing Mufasa over you."

"Yeah, yeah," Banzai said nervously. "He's always playing favorites."

"Hee-hee-hee," said Ed.

"So what?" Taka growled.

"It's just . . . well, I'd want to get even if I were you, that's all." Shenzi sounded scared.

"I will." Taka put his face close to hers. "I'm going hunting with Mufasa. I'll show him up by bringing back some big game. Then my father will realize Mufasa isn't perfect."

Shenzi was licking her lips. "That's nice and all, but why not do something that makes Mufasa look bad? Maybe Ahadi will realize you should be the next

Lion King instead of your brother."

Ed joggled his head in agreement.

"Yeah," Banzai said. "If Mufasa looks like a loser, you'll look good."

Taka raised an eyebrow. "I'll let that one go," he said. "But Shenzi's idea appeals to me. What terrible deed should it be? Mufasa would have to break a law of the land to cause our father to lose faith in him."

"You mean like killing for sport?" Banzai asked.

"Something like that." Taka grinned. "If some of the animals began fighting because of something Mufasa did," Taka said, "the other animals would lose faith in their ruler and his firstborn son."

"Do you have a plan?" Shenzi asked.

"A plan is coming to me."

"You won't forget about sharing that big game, will you?" Shenzi asked.

Taka laughed. "Such simple creatures." He turned to leave. "You'll have your eats, and your fun too."

From his hiding place in the tree, Rafiki watched Taka race back the way they had come. The moment the hyenas left, he followed Taka. Moving as fast as he could, he leaped from limb to limb, high above the ground.

Rafiki kept thinking about the cobra in his bed, and the look of hate in Taka's eyes when he had talked of getting even. How far would he go? Rafiki wondered.

Rafiki should have kept his mind on what he was doing. The drought and days of scorching sun had done their work well. A limb cracked. Terror flashed through Rafiki as he fell to the ground far below.

There was a moment of terrible pain, then the sky, trees, and earth swirled into darkness.

CHAPTER 6

The first thing Rafiki heard was the wind in the trees. It was rather soothing. Then a high-pitched voice jolted him upright.

"A simian your age should not be flying through the trees like a youngster."

It was Zuzu. She was standing on the ground near Rafiki, shaking her head. "You are so lucky you didn't break anything, and that I was flying by, and that I saw you, and—"

"Thank you for your help," Rafiki said.

With Zuzu's aid, Rafiki struggled to his feet. "Have I been lying here long?"

"Not really," she said.

But it was long enough for Taka to cover a great distance, Rafiki realized. How would he ever find him? Then he remembered Zuzu's morning exercise flights with her family. "We see everything," she'd said.

"Have you seen Taka, Mufasa, or the Lion King?" Rafiki asked.

"Ahadi is over at the elephant burial grounds," she said, brushing off Rafiki's fur. "The hyenas hide out there from time to time. I haven't seen Taka," she muttered. "But I saw Mufasa headed toward Five Stones."

"Please find the Lion King and ask him to search for his sons," Rafiki begged Zuzu. "It's urgent."

"Where?"

"Tell him to start at Five Stones," he said.

Zuzu nodded, took to the sky, and was gone.

This time, Rafiki ran along the plain. Over rocks, across dry, cracked earth, and through bushes filled with thorns.

At Five Stones, Mufasa was nowhere in sight, but Rafiki caught his scent in the air.

He could also smell Taka.

Rafiki frantically searched the ground until he found their trail, and followed it as quickly as he could.

They were running. Rafiki could tell by the length of the stride. And they were covering a great deal of distance. What was Taka's plan? Where was he taking his brother?

Their trail led to the top of a hill. Rafiki stopped to catch his breath. Far below, he could see a pool of water. The last water hole, he realized.

Standing in the pool up to his belly was the largest Cape buffalo Rafiki had ever seen. And creeping toward the pool was Mufasa. He wasn't stalking the buffalo, but he was being cautious.

Taka was nowhere in sight.

Rafiki ran down the hill and caught up

with Mufasa just as he got to the pond.

The buffalo glared at them. His thick brow twisted into a deep scowl under his long, curved horns.

"What are you doing here?" Rafiki asked Mufasa.

"I'm helping my father," he said. "If we can get Boma to agree to share the water, it will be better for all the animals."

"That's only fair," Rafiki said. "But Boma doesn't look like—" A terrible thought struck Rafiki. "What do you mean, we?" he asked.

"Taka and I," Mufasa replied. "It was his idea."

"Then, where is he?" Rafiki glanced around and saw Taka in the grass at the edge of the pool.

"What do you want, Mufasa?" Boma's voice was as deep as the rumbling earth.

Mufasa swallowed hard. "I want to talk to you about this water hole. You must share it with the other animals

until the rains come."

"Must I?" Boma raised his head.

Taka came out of the grass at the edge of the pool behind Boma and roared.

Boma whirled around.

"Taka, what are you doing?" Mufasa called.

"Enforcing the Lion King's orders," Taka yelled. "Boma"—Taka snarled at the buffalo—"you will share this water hole or face my brother in combat!" There was a smirk on Taka's face.

"So, Ahadi sends his children to me!" Boma's voice boomed like thunder. He turned to Mufasa. "And you want to fight me!"

"No, I—"

"Very well, then!" Boma lowered his head. "Let the fight begin!" He charged out of the water.

"Run, Mufasa!" Rafiki shouted.

"But I—"

The earth trembled under Boma's hooves.

"Run!" Rafiki yelled again.

Mufasa and Rafiki ran as fast as they could. Yet Rafiki could feel the great buffalo closing in on them.

Zuzu is right, Rafiki thought. I am getting too old for this. But if Boma has his way, I will never have to do it again.

CHAPTER 7

Boma was getting closer when
Mufasa turned to the right. "This
way!" he yelled.

The ground slanted downward.
Mufasa ran along a path that led into a
large rock formation.

Rafiki followed him, and so did Boma.

"Run, coward!" Boma bellowed.

Rafiki's chest and legs hurt, and he was
having trouble breathing. The fall and the
miles he had run were catching up with
him. Soon, he wouldn't be able to run at
all.

Up ahead, a log lay across the path.

"I'll never make it," Rafiki told

Mufasa. "Go on without me."

"Jump on my back!" Mufasa shouted.

"That will slow you down," Rafiki said.

"Jump on!" Mufasa commanded.

Rafiki hopped aboard. Mufasa was born to be a king. His muscles bulged with the effort to maintain his speed and carry the baboon. But he managed to do both.

"You'll never make it around that log," Rafiki warned Mufasa. "Boma is too close."

"Don't need to," Mufasa said.

Mufasa sprang up onto the log. With a push from his powerful hind legs, he and Rafiki shot out into the air.

Rafiki saw what Mufasa's plan was. There was a ravine just beyond the log. Mufasa's leap brought them down on the far side of the ravine.

Boma bounded over the log. His eyes went wide with shock. He fell into the ravine with a loud crash.

Mufasa skidded to a stop. "I once fell in there myself," he told Boma.

"I'll get you for this!" Boma yelled.

Mufasa sighed. "I didn't come to fight you. We are all brothers. Brothers in the circle of life."

But Boma wasn't listening. "I'll get you, and the others will get your brother!"

"The others?" Mufasa asked. He and

Rafiki scrambled to the top of a cluster of rocks. In the distance, near the water hole, Taka was rolling on the ground with laughter. Three large buffaloes burst from the tall yellow grass. Of course, thought Rafiki, buffaloes travel in herds.

"My brother!" Mufasa screamed.

Taka started running, but the buffaloes were already closing in on him.

"I've got to help him!" Mufasa ran

down the rocks. He leaped across the ravine onto the log and ran back up the path.

"They'll trample you too!" Rafiki yelled. But Mufasa didn't stop.

"Help me! Help me!" Taka screamed. He twisted left, then right, trying to get away. But the buffaloes stayed with him, slashing at him with their horns.

Taka stumbled, and the biggest buffalo struck him with one of his sharp, curved horns. Taka fell to the ground and rolled a few feet. After that, he didn't move at all.

The buffaloes paused, pawing the ground.

Mufasa reached Taka's side. Standing between him and the buffaloes, Mufasa roared and readied himself for the fight. A fight he couldn't possibly win.

The buffaloes lowered their heads, preparing to charge.

A trumpeting sound startled everyone. Looking to the left, Rafiki saw Ahadi leading a charge of elephants and other animals. They raced down the hill and surrounded the buffaloes and the young lions.

"I got them here as fast as I could." Zuzu landed on the log beside Rafiki. "You look terrible."

Rafiki smiled at her. "And you look beautiful." She buried her head in her feathers.

Still winded, Rafiki joined the king and the others.

"How dare you attack my sons!" Ahadi roared.

"Well, they started it," one of the buffaloes whined.

"It's a long story," Rafiki told Ahadi.

Mufasa ran up to his father. "Taka is hurt," he said. "I can't get him to move."

CHAPTER 8

I will look after him," Rafiki said.

Ahadi turned to the buffaloes. "You'd better hope it's not serious," he growled. Then he joined Mufasa and Rafiki.

"There are no broken bones," Rafiki told Ahadi after he had examined Taka. "But he has a deep cut on his face." Taka moaned, and Ahadi nuzzled him.

"I have some herbs in my pouch back at Pride Rock," Rafiki said. "They will help."

"Then let's take him home." Ahadi asked one of the elephants to lift Taka in his trunk. The king sent another elephant to help Boma out of the gully. Then Rafiki and the lions went back to Pride Rock, leading the elephant who carried Taka.

"You'll be sore for a few days," Rafiki told Taka later. "And you will carry that scar for the rest of your life."

"It will serve as a reminder of how reckless you were," Ahadi said.

"Why did you make Boma angry?" Mufasa asked his brother.

"To embarrass you," Taka replied. "And to get even with Father for breaking his promise!"

"Instead of hurting us, you nearly got yourself killed," Ahadi said. "You must rid yourself of the anger that rules you, my son. Perhaps the wound you received will serve as a reminder of this."

Taka's eyes filled with anger, then grew calm and clear. "That's right." He gave Mufasa a half smile. "From now on, call me Scar. Father, I won't forget what happened today. I promise."

Mufasa, Ahadi, and Rafiki went to join Zuzu, who was waiting for them.

"In spite of Taka's attack, Boma and his herd have promised to let the other animals share the water," Ahadi said. "That will ease the crisis. Tomorrow, I'll deal with the hyenas." He sighed. "If only I could learn of such problems before they grew into crises!"

"You can," Rafiki told the king. "Appoint someone to be your eyes and ears in the kingdom. Someone who will help you stay in touch with your subjects."

"A good idea," said Ahadi. "But who?"

"Zuzu would be my first choice," Rafiki said. "If not for her, things would have ended much differently today."

"Would you take the job, Zuzu?" Ahadi asked.

Zuzu's feathers puffed out with pride. "Yes, Your Majesty."

"So be it!" Ahadi proclaimed. "From

this day forward, you and your family shall be stewards to the kings of the Pride Lands."

Zuzu bowed, then took to the air. "I must go tell my family. My son will be so proud."

"And you, wise Rafiki," Ahadi continued, "shall be my teacher."

Now Rafiki was the one who was embarrassed. "Your Majesty, I cannot stay—"

Ahadi smiled. "Rafiki, I want to make the Pride Lands a place where all animals can thrive. This will be possible if we cooperate. Will you help us achieve that goal?"

Rafiki was speechless. He was used to being alone.

"Yes, I will!" he finally decided. "As long as I can go off on my quests from time to time. There is so much I wish to learn."

"So be it!" Ahadi rose and gazed out over the moonlit plain. "I can feel it," he

said. "This is the beginning of a great era for all of us under the stars."

Rafiki opened his eyes. Kopa was sitting wide-eyed near Simba and Nala.

"It rained a few weeks later, ending the drought," Rafiki said, concluding his story.

"Wow!" said Kopa. "Grandfather and Great-grandfather were really something."

"That they were," Rafiki agreed. "So was your great-grandmother, Uru. She discovered a lake at the western edge of the Pride Lands, and many animals were saved from thirst."

Zazu puffed out his chest. "I remember the day my mother came home and told us about her new position with the Lion King." He smiled. "She was right. We were all very proud."

"And you have served the kings well ever since," Simba said.

"Wow! That was a great story." Kopa

thought for a moment. "Great-uncle Scar was a real creep."

"Kopa," Nala said.

"Well, he was," Kopa mumbled.

Simba turned to Rafiki. "Thank you for the tale," he said. "It has taught me a great deal."

"Me too," said Kopa.

"It has reminded me how much went into making this land what it is." Simba brushed Nala with his nose, then nuzzled Kopa. "It's also reminded me how important our loved ones are. And the importance of a promise. The path of the son begins with the steps of the father."

Kopa jumped up and down. "You mean?"

"I will deal with the problem at the water hole right after I take my son and my mate to the top of Pride Rock."

"All right!" Kopa cheered.

"After all," Simba said, "it's a tradition."

Rafiki smiled. "And a wise one at that."